Shark and Crab

written by Julie Ellis
illustrated by Kelvin Hawley

1

One day a hungry shark was
looking for something to eat.
He saw a little crab.

"Don't eat me," said the crab.
"I could help you one day."
"How could a little crab
help me?" said the shark.

The shark let the crab go.
He saw some little fish.
"I will eat all the fish,"
he said.

The hungry shark was looking
at the little fish.
He didn't see a big net
coming down in the water.

The fish swam into the net.
The shark swam after them.
He went into the net, too.

The shark couldn't swim away.
"Help! Help!" he shouted.
"I can't get out of the net!"

All the little fish swam
out of the net.
But the shark was too big.

He couldn't swim out.
"Help! Help!" he shouted.
"How can I get out?"

The net was going up out
of the water.
The shark was going up, too.

"Help me!" he shouted.
"I'm going up in the net!
Come and help me!"

The little crab saw the shark
going up in the net.
"I could help you," he said.

"You didn't eat me.
You let me go," said the crab.
"I'm coming to help you."

The crab went Snip! Snip!
He made a little hole
in the net.

Snip! Snip! The hole got big.
The shark swam out of
the hole.

"Thank you," said the shark.
"A little crab could help
me after all."